THE
MISSION POSSIBLE MYSTERY
AT

Space
Center
Houston

First Edition ©2009 Carole Marsh/Gallopade International/Peachtree City, GA
Current Edition ©August 2015
Ebook Edition ©2011
All rights reserved.
Manufactured in Peachtree City, GA

Carole Marsh Mysteries™ and its skull colophon are the property of Carole Marsh and Gallopade International.

Published by Gallopade International/Carole Marsh Books. Printed in the United States of America.

Managing Editor: Sherry Moss
Senior Editor: Aimee Holden
Assistant Editor: Susan Walworth
Cover Design: Vicki DeJoy
Cover Photo Credits: NASA
Picture Credits: Vicki DeJoy
Content Design and Illustrations: Lisa Stanley

Gallopade International is introducing SAT words that kids need to know in each new book that we publish. The SAT words are bold in the story. Look for this special logo beside each word in the glossary. Happy Learning!

Gallopade is proud to be a member and supporter of these educational organizations and associations:

American Booksellers Association
American Library Association
International Reading Association
National Association for Gifted Children
The National School Supply and Equipment Association
The National Council for the Social Studies
Museum Store Association
Association of Partners for Public Lands
Association of Booksellers for Children
Association for the Study of African American Life and History
National Alliance of Black School Educators

Once upon a time...

Hmm, kids keep asking me to write a mystery book. What shall I do?

Mimi

Write one about spiders!

Papa said ...

Why don't you set the stories in real locations?

That's a great idea! And if I do that, I might as well choose real kids as characters in the stories! But which kids would I pick?

MIMI, PICK ME, PICK ME!

ME, TOO, MIMI, PICK ME, TOO!

Christina

Grant

Pick me!

You two really are characters, that's all I've got to say!

Yes you are! And, of course I choose you! But what should I write about?

 National Parks!

SCARY PLACES!

Famous Places!

FUN PLACES!

Disney World!

 New York City!

Dracula's Castle

 **GRAND CANYON**

On the *Mystery Girl* airplane ...

I CAN FLY US ANYWHERE!

Mystery Girl

Or aboard
the *Mimi!*

Mimi

Take me to the
Forbidden City!

Or by surfboard,
rickshaw,
motorbike,
camel ...

All great ideas!
I can put a lot of history,
MYSTERY,
legend, lore, and laughs in
the books! We can use other boys and girls
in the books. It will be educational and fun!

Good
stuff!

Where will you get the other kids, Mimi?

From my Fan Club! Kids can apply to be characters!

And can you put some cool stuff online? Like a Book Club and a Scavenger Hunt and a Map so we can track our adventures?

Of course!

And can cousins Avery and Ella and Evan and some of our friends be in the books?

Of course!

Can I apply?

9

And so, Mimi, Papa, Christina, and Grant took off aboard the *Mystery Girl* and America's National Mystery Book Series—where the adventure is real and so are the characters! —was born.

START YOUR ADVENTURE TODAY!

READ THE BOOK!

GO ONLINE!

TRACK YOUR ADVENTURES!

APPLY TO BE A CHARACTER!

Yikes! That was close!

Rats!

ABOUT THE CHARACTERS

Christina
Yother
Age 10

Grant
Yother
Age 7

Junko
Minari
Age 10

Phillip
Smith
Age 8

1
COUNTDOWN CONFUSION

Christina tried to wiggle, but the seat belt held her tighter than her grandmother's hugs. Instead, she focused on the colorful blinking lights of the console before her.

"There's no backing out now," she mumbled. Biting the corner of her lip, she feared that this time her curiosity had gotten her in over her head.

A deep voice startled her. "TEN. NINE. EIGHT. SEVEN. WE HAVE A GO FOR MAIN ENGINE START..."

Colossal engines roared to life and Christina's fingertips dug into the arms of her seat as it began to vibrate.

"SIX. FIVE. FOUR. THREE. TWO. ONE. ZERO. WE HAVE BOOSTER IGNITION AND LIFTOFF OF THE SPACE SHUTTLE EXPLORER!"

The shuttle broke free from the launch pad like a wild bull breaking out of a rodeo chute. And Christina was its rider! Every bone in her body *sh-sh*-shook and her teeth *ch-ch*-chattered.

"HOUSTON NOW CONTROLLING THE FLIGHT OF SPACE SHUTTLE EXPLORER..." the voice said. "WE HAVE NEW RESIDENTS HEADED FOR THE INTERNATIONAL SPACE STATION..."

Christina had always wondered how astronauts felt when they launched into space for the first time. Now she knew. It was scary, but exciting!

She tried to turn her head to see how her younger brother Grant and her grandparents Mimi and Papa were handling their own fear and excitement, but the powerful force of shooting into space kept her pinned firmly to her seat. Her cheeks felt like pancakes.

Christina had traveled the world with her brother and grandparents, but she never dreamed this trip would be so *out of this world!*

"SHUTTLE COMPLETING ITS ROLL FOR THE EIGHT AND A HALF MINUTE

RIDE TO ORBIT," the voice announced as Christina's stomach

then

"THREE LIQUID FUEL MAIN ENGINES NOW THROTTLING BACK TO REDUCE THE STRESS ON THE SHUTTLE AS IT BREAKS THROUGH THE SOUND BARRIER..."

Christina couldn't believe her ears. She was traveling faster than sound! Her numb fingers slowly relaxed their grip as the shuttle ride became smooth—almost as smooth as cruising down the interstate in Mimi's and Papa's little red convertible.

"SHUTTLE, THIS IS HOUSTON, GO AT THROTTLE UP..." the voice said.

For the first time, Christina heard the shuttle commander's reply. "Go at throttle up," he answered.

The voice continued, "SHUTTLE ALREADY ELEVEN AND A HALF MILES IN ALTITUDE, EIGHT MILES DOWN RANGE FROM THE KENNEDY SPACE CENTER...SHUTTLE TRAVELING ALMOST 2,400 MILES PER HOUR...STANDING BY FOR SOLID ROCKET BOOSTER SEPARATION..."

A blinding

filled the windows and the shuttle lurched like a

car hitting a speed bump as the rocket boosters separated and fell back to Earth.

The shuttle commander spoke again. "Congratulations! We are at 50 nautical miles and you are now officially astronauts!"

The brilliant blue sky was turning black as night. The squeezing force slowly released her, and Christina felt her arms get lighter and lighter until they floated.

"The space shuttle is now 214 miles above the South Pacific Ocean—next stop, International Space Station," the shuttle commander announced.

Suddenly, Christina wondered if the shuttle had brakes. "Will we slow down in time?" she worried. "Or will we have a space fender-bender?!"

2
MISSING MOON

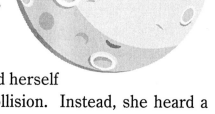

"The shuttle is now traveling 17,000 miles per hour. Prepare to dock International Space Station..." the commander announced.

Christina braced herself for an explosive collision. Instead, she heard a loud CLANK and CLICK.

"Docking is complete," the commander said. "Welcome to the International Space Station, astronauts!"

SWISH!

Doors flew open. People unbuckled their seatbelts. A firm tap on her shoulder made Christina jump.

"Snap out of it!" Papa said. "The simulation ride is over."

Grant pushed past her seat. "That was awesome!" he said. "Now I understand what a simulation ride is. It makes you feel like you're really there!"

The simulation was so real to Christina that she found it difficult to return to reality. She wished she was really on the Space Station.

"Was the simulation as exciting as you imagined it would be?" Mimi asked, wrapping an arm around her starry-eyed granddaughter's trembling shoulders.

"More exciting!" Christina said as they exited the Blast Off Theater at Space Center Houston, the official visitor's center of the Johnson Space Center in Houston, Texas. "I could see myself becoming an astronaut!"

"I remember that feeling," Mimi said. "There was nothing like eating dinner on a TV tray and watching snowy pictures of Neil Armstrong take those first steps on the moon."

Grant looked confused. "I think your memory's bad about the snow," he said. "There's no snow on the moon."

"Of course not," Mimi replied. "I meant that the black and white TV picture wasn't good so it looked like snow. Technology wasn't as advanced then. We couldn't get crystal clear pictures from space like we do now."

Papa helped Mimi with the history lesson. "President John F. Kennedy said in 1961 that he wanted the United States to put a man on the moon by the end of the decade. Neil Armstrong became the first human to set foot on the moon after he and Buzz Aldrin landed the *Apollo 11* there in 1969."

"Oh!" Christina said excitedly. "Was he the guy who said, 'One small step for man; one giant leap for mankind?'"

"That's right, Christina!" Mimi exclaimed. "And don't forget it was a group of NASA scientists and engineers right here at Johnson

Space Center who helped those men reach the moon. That's why they call it the 'home of human space flight.'"

"What does NASA mean?" Grant asked.

"NASA stands for National Aeronautics and Space Administration," Christina explained, proud that she knew more than her little brother. "Did you want to be an astronaut?" she asked Mimi.

"No," Mimi said. "But I was so impressed with the images of the moon and space that I wanted to be an astronomer."

"That's funny!" Grant said with a giggle. "You wanted to be an astronomer and you became a mystery writer."

"At least I can write about space," Mimi said. "Who knows? I might write a space mystery after this visit!"

Christina's eyes roamed the cavernous Space Center with all its exhibits and activities. She didn't know what to look at first.

This was a visit Christina and Grant had anticipated for months. When an old friend, Judy, and her husband, Kent, invited Mimi and

Papa to visit their Houston ranch, Mimi eagerly accepted. There was no way she could **oppose** her grandkids, who begged to come along and learn about space exploration.

"You're out of this world!" Christina joked when Mimi finally said OK.

The always impatient Grant spotted something that snatched his attention. "What are those rocks doing here?" he asked.

"I'll bet those are moon rocks!" Papa said, racing Grant to the display.

Grant rubbed his fingers across a piece of gray rock as rough as the sandpaper in Papa's toolbox. "I have touched the moon!" he shouted triumphantly.

Other rocks reclined like creepy alien lumps in a long glass case. Attached to holes in the side were black rubber gloves.

"What are those gloves for?" asked Grant.

"To take the rocks in and out," Mimi answered. "Those rocks are very valuable."

"It says here that only 840 pounds of rocks have been brought back from the moon," Christina read.

"When moon rocks were first brought back to Earth, people were afraid they might contain dangerous germs," said Papa.

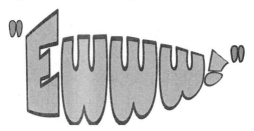

"No wonder you need to wear gloves!" Grant said, wiping his hands on his pants like they were crawling with moon cooties. "Gross!"

"Don't worry," Mimi said, laughing. "Scientists never found any germs."

Christina found one rock particularly interesting. About the size of a lumpy softball, it was a lava rock from a volcanic eruption. In 1971, *Apollo 15* astronauts collected it near the crest of Dune Crater. Somehow, it looked familiar.

"Hey Grant, this looks just like your nose," she said and laughed. "There's even a booger coming out!"

What are those rocks doing here?

"Ha, ha," Grant said, rolling his eyes. "You're very scientific. I'm going to look at space suits."

Christina followed Grant into the Astronaut Gallery where photos of every astronaut who had flown in space lined the walls. Space movie theme songs poured from speakers and inspired Grant to become Hero Spaceman. With one fist on his hip and the other aimed for the stars, he shouted, "To infinity and beyond!"

Large glass tubes held spacesuits that stood at attention as if waiting for their next mission. Some were silver, but most were white and puffy.

"They look like marshmallow men!" Christina observed.

"Are there astronauts inside these?" Grant asked, with a puzzled expression.

It was Christina's turn to roll her eyes. "Grant, can't you imagine astronauts have better things to do than stand around on display?" she asked.

"Then why did this one just *m-m*-move?" Grant asked with a quivering voice.

"You're just spacey, Grant," Christina said, moving down the line to admire a suit with a gold face shield as shiny as a mirror. She noticed her hair sticking up and was about to smooth it down when the face shield reflected a gang of security guards galloping by.

"What's going on?" she asked a young boy standing beside her.

"Someone said one of the moon rocks has been stolen!" he whispered.

3
SUITABLE SUSPECT

Grant's mouth flew open after Christina ran back to tell him about the stolen moon rock.

"I didn't do it!" he exclaimed. "I was just looking at the moon rocks—honest!"

"Calm down, Grant!" Christina commanded, flicking her brown hair off her shoulder and scratching the back of her neck. It was an itch she always got when she sensed a mystery, and this one was a humdinger.

"I seriously doubt a tourist could steal one of the moon rocks," Christina said thoughtfully. "A crime like that would have to be an inside job."

"Duh," Grant said. "Does it look like we're outside?"

"No," Christina said. "I mean that someone who works here probably had something to do with the crime since there's so much security."

"Maybe the thief was hiding in the spacesuit I saw move," Grant suggested.

Christina didn't want to admit the possibility that they could have been standing next to a dangerous crook. But her neck was awfully itchy.

The boy Christina had talked to had wandered close and was eavesdropping on their conversation.

Grant looked at him suspiciously. "Do you work here?" he asked.

"Nope," the boy answered.

"Whew!" Grant exclaimed, wiping sweat from his forehead. "I was afraid you might be the rock thief."

"I'm Phillip," he said. "I'm going to be an astronaut!"

"You mean when you grow up?" Grant asked.

"No," he replied. "Tomorrow. I'm coming to space camp while my mother attends a conference."

"Do you think Mimi and Papa would let us go to space camp too, Christina?" Grant asked.

"What better way to solve a moon rock mystery?" Christina said. "We'll try and convince them on the way to the ranch."

"Great!" Phillip said.

" YIKES! "

Christina yelped, and jumped when Mimi grabbed her from behind. The thought of a crook creeping around the place had her nerves on edge.

"Come quick!" Mimi said, waving frantically for them to follow her to a helmet display. "You've got to see this!"

Papa was forcing a clear, bubble-shaped helmet over his gray hair. Christina laughed at the sight of her tall grandfather in his leather vest and cowboy boots wearing a space helmet. "You look like a space cowboy!" she exclaimed.

"You kids ready to blast off to another display?" Papa asked. Through the helmet, his deep voice sounded like Darth Vader.

"Hope to see you tomorrow!" Christina and Grant said, waving goodbye to Phillip. When they passed the moon rock display, Christina was shocked to see which one was missing. It was Grant's nose rock!

"Why that one?" Christina muttered to herself as something else caught her eye. A crumpled piece of yellow paper looked out of place on the shiny floor. She picked it up, but before she could unfold it, a man in a blue jumpsuit breezed by.

"I'll take that!" he said cheerfully.

"Thank you," Christina replied politely, thinking he must be a custodian. But she really hadn't wanted to part with the paper since it could be a clue! Maybe that's why she had gripped it so tight that a small piece tore off when she handed it over.

PLANET

When she opened her hand, Christina saw the word PLANET scribbled on the jagged yellow square stuck to her thumb.

4
SPACE AND SPURS

"That hurts, Grant!" Christina yelled, swatting at her little brother's newest toy. "Papa, why did you buy this robot claw for Grant? All he's done is pinch me with it since we got in the car!"

"I should have bought one for you so it would be a fair fight," Papa said.

Christina had made a wiser choice at the Space Center gift shop—a space pen that wrote upside down. Holding the Texas map against the ceiling of the rental car, she traced their route to the ranch.

"Why don't you try these snacks, instead of pinching your sister?" Mimi asked Grant. She had bought them freeze-dried ice cream sandwiches and space food sticks like the astronauts eat during space missions.

"I'm saving them to take to school when I get home," Grant answered. "I'll be the only kid with space snacks. How much longer 'til we see some real Texas stuff?" he asked impatiently.

When they landed in Houston, Grant had expected to see cowboys driving dusty herds of longhorn cattle. Instead, they were speeding down a modern interstate in a maze of roads that reminded Christina of spaghetti.

Glancing out the window as they sped over a high overpass, Christina couldn't believe what she saw sparkling in the sunlight.

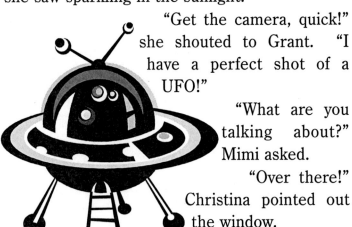

"Get the camera, quick!" she shouted to Grant. "I have a perfect shot of a UFO!"

"What are you talking about?" Mimi asked.

"Over there!" Christina pointed out the window.

Mimi shielded her blue eyes from the afternoon sun. "That's no UFO!" she said, and laughed. "That's the Astrodome."

"I saw the Houston Astros play the New York Yankees there," Papa added.

"Alright, what's the Astrodome?" Christina asked, leaning back in the seat.

Mimi explained, "That giant round building with the UFO-shaped roof was the first domed sports arena in the world. It was built so people could watch baseball no matter what the weather was like. When it opened, it was nicknamed the Eighth Wonder of the World."

Papa piped in, "The best part about the Astrodome is that they never have to water or cut the grass!"

"Why?" Grant asked.

"Ever heard of Astroturf?" he questioned.

"Sure," said Grant. "It's that fake grass on the putt-putt golf course."

"It got its name from the Astrodome," Papa explained. "Baseball players complained the sunlight needed for real grass blinded them, so they installed fake stuff."

The gleaming skyscrapers of Houston had grown small behind them when Grant noticed another unusual object. "Someone's making a statue of a praying mantis," he said. "It's even moving!"

"That's no statue," Christina corrected. "That's an oil well. Houston is famous for energy production. I read that oil was discovered here in 1901."

"Why didn't they name the town Oilville?" asked Grant.

"Houston got its name from General Sam Houston who helped Texas win its independence from Mexico in 1836," Mimi said. "Texas was a country then and Sam Houston was named its president. It didn't become the 28th state until 1846. Since then it's grown from a railroad spur where cattle were loaded onto trains to the home of space travel."

Grant let down the car window and hot wind tousled his unruly blonde curls. "Nothing like breathing in the wide open spaces!" he exclaimed. Suddenly, his nose crinkled. "It doesn't smell as fresh as I expected. In fact, it smells sort of poopy."

"That's those longhorns you wanted to see, or should I say smell?" Christina said, and giggled.

Finally, Papa turned into a long driveway. The sky had quickly changed from blue to an ominous red. Hot wind whipped up thick clouds of dust.

Christina squinted to see a weathered sign.

Nailed to it was a ghostly-white cow skull with long, pointed horns that shook violently in the wind and stared at her with angry eyes.

"What are those?" Grant screeched. He wasn't talking about the cow horns. Shadowy orbs raced toward the car. Christina gasped as the mysterious objects scratched on her window like skeleton hands.

"Relax, guys," Mimi reassured them. "This storm has unleashed a bunch of tumbleweeds and they're blowing against the car."

"Are you sure this is the right ranch?" Christina asked nervously. "It doesn't seem as friendly as I had pictured."

"Here comes something else," Grant yelped. "And it's no tumbleweed!"

Christina watched a dark figure grow larger and larger until a man on a black horse appeared out of the dust. He wore a red bandana across his nose and mouth.

"Papa, it's a holdup!" Grant cried.

5
LONG HORNS
AND POINTED TOES

The mysterious horseman waved for them to follow him through the blinding dust. Soon they were in front of an enormous, log ranch house.

"Let's make a run for it!" Papa said, leading the way to the front door.

They all stumbled inside, coughing on the dust that clogged their throats.

"Don't do that, Grant!" Christina said when she saw her brother picking his nose.

"It's full of dirt!" he whined.

Mimi's friend Judy rushed in with tall glasses of ice water and sympathetic hugs. "Sorry ya'll had to blow in on a dust storm," she said. "I'm glad Kent found you!"

Judy was a pretty blonde like Mimi. They laughed when they realized they were both dressed in jeans, red plaid shirts, and red cowboy boots.

Kent came in slapping the dust off his cowboy boots with his bandana. They were the fanciest boots Christina had ever seen—ostrich skin with gold metal caps on the pointed toes.

"I like your boots," she said.

"Had 'em custom made," Kent answered in a Texas drawl as thick as syrup. "I hope you kids like the ranch. Every time our grandkids come, all they want to do is go to space camp."

Christina gave Mimi a pleading look.

"OK," Mimi said. "Papa can drive you back in the morning, as long as you're here for the big Texas barbecue Judy has planned!"

When Christina turned to give Grant a high-five, he wasn't there. She found him prowling around Kent's office.

"Awesome!" Grant said, marveling at walls decorated with shaggy buffalo heads, deer antlers, the long horns of a Texas steer, and even a mounted armadillo. He rubbed the armadillo's rough shell. "I've never seen one that wasn't road-kill!" he said, plopping down in

the throne-sized leather chair behind the desk.
It protested with a loud

SQUEEEEK!

"Wonder what this is for?" Christina asked,
eyeing an empty metal stand on the desk.

"I bet there are some cool things in these
desk drawers, too!" Grant said, giving each one
a pull.

"Grant, you know better than to go
rummaging through someone's desk," Christina
scolded.

"No use," Grant said. "They're all locked."

*Hmmm—a peculiar empty stand and a locked
desk,* Christina thought. *Does Kent have
something to hide?*

6
NASA
KNOW-IT-ALL

Early the next morning, Grant scanned the sea of kids at space camp and finally spotted Phillip. "Hey! Phillip!" he shouted, and dashed across the polished floor of Space Center Houston.

Christina watched in horror. Grant was flying through the air as if the gravitational pull of Earth had suddenly been switched off.

"You should watch where you're going!" a girl about Christina's age hollered.

"You shouldn't stop and bend over in the middle of a busy place!" Grant protested.

"I was tying my shoe so I wouldn't trip!" the girl fussed. She gathered her bags that had skittered across the floor.

"You weren't worried about making me trip," Grant argued.

"WHOA!" Christina shouted to stop the bickering. "Let's rewind and start over. I'm Christina. This is my sometimes **clumsy** brother, Grant. We're here for space camp."

"I'm Junko," the girl replied. She pulled her long, shiny black hair into a ponytail. "Unfortunately, I'll see more of your clumsy brother since I'm going to space camp, too."

The kids joined the line of campers dragging gear they needed for the two-day, overnight camp. Grant finally caught Phillip's attention and quickly moved beside him.

"Did you hear about the stolen moon rock?" Christina asked Junko.

"Of course I did," Junko answered abruptly. "There's not much that happens around NASA that I don't know about."

Christina didn't like her attitude. "Do you also know who took it?" she asked.

"I don't know yet," Junko answered. "No one does. But most of the security people think it's an inside job."

We're going to space camp!

"I think so, too," Christina agreed excitedly. "I can't imagine how anyone could have taken the moon rock from such a busy place, especially without triggering alarms."

Christina was about to ask Junko how she knew so much about Space Center Houston, when the camp counselor whistled for attention. He was tall and thin with bushy hair that hung down to his eyebrows. A red backpack hung limply over one shoulder. Christina thought he might be a college student.

"My name's Todd," he said nervously. "Stash your gear quickly and meet in the Gallery of Planets. If we're going to be astronauts, we have to learn about what's in space."

"Thrill, thrill," Junko said, and yawned as the counselor left. "I've been through the Gallery of Planets a thousand times."

The talk of planets jogged Christina's memory. The word PLANET

was all she had from the possible clue the man in the blue jumpsuit snatched from her hand. Was it enough to launch them on a galactic adventure to catch a thief?

7
RACE ME TO THE MOON

A chill climbed Christina's bare arms and told her she should have worn a sweater in the dark Gallery of Planets. Once again, she imagined herself as an astronaut, taking a space walk past the solar system's colorful giants.

Christina stared at soft-looking Jupiter. Lines of cream and reddish-brown circled the planet, along with occasional blobs of color. It reminded Christina of her favorite ice cream, Neapolitan, when the vanilla, chocolate, and strawberry melted together to make a kaleidoscope of colors.

Grant and Phillip found an activity that controlled two planets' rotations with handles. Soon, it became a race. Faster and faster they turned the handles until Grant was red-faced with effort. His tongue stuck firmly out of the corner of his mouth, a sure sign to Christina that he was giving his all.

"Stop that, Grant!" Christina ordered from across Jupiter. He didn't have time to obey. She watched Grant's planet jump out of the display and roll down the plaza like a bowling ball.

"Watch out!" Grant yelled, as he chased the celestial ball.

Christina's chill turned to sweat when she saw it heading straight for Junko.

The runaway planet hit the tattered tennis shoe of Todd, the camp counselor, launched, and smacked Junko in the stomach, knocking her on her bottom.

"Where in the world did that come from?" Todd asked angrily.

Junko, more embarrassed than hurt, pointed an accusing finger at Grant. "I'm sure he had something to do with it!" she said.

As annoying and clumsy as her little brother could be sometimes, Christina knew he didn't mean any harm. "He was trying to catch it!" she said in his defense.

"Well, you need to hold his hand and keep him out of trouble!" Junko demanded.

Spinning away from Junko, Christina told Grant and Phillip, "Come on guys, let's go and explore Saturn."

"Roger!" Grant said. "That means OK in astronaut language."

"I know, Grant," Christina said with a sigh.

Christina considered Saturn, the jewel of the solar system, her favorite planet. "Don't you think it looks mysterious?" she asked the boys. She admired its colors—bands of lavender, spring green, yellow, gray-blue, and reddish-brown.

"Oh, this is the married planet!" Grant said. He had quickly recovered from his latest embarrassment.

"The married planet?" asked Phillip.

"Yeah, it has a ring!" Grant said, and laughed heartily at his own joke. "Got you with that one, didn't I!"

Phillip smiled good-naturedly at the corny joke. Christina wished Junko could feel the same way about Grant.

The beautiful, rotating orb was mesmerizing, until Christina noticed something odd underneath the rings.

"Look between those bands of color under the rings," she said. "I swear I could see writing."

The boys waited patiently for the planet to make another turn. They were able to make out the letters

MGA.

"That doesn't spell anything," Christina said. "But during the next rotation they read RACE ME TO THE MOON."

"Maybe that's the company that created the exhibit," Phillip suggested.

"Maybe," Christina agreed. "But remember those words. When you're solving mysteries, you don't take anything for granted."

Christina was already thinking ahead. *If this was a clue, did they have the right stuff to win a space race?* She glanced over at Grant and was shocked to see him holding his throat. His face was redder than Mimi's favorite hat.

"Help me!" Grant gasped. "I can't breathe!"

8
TANG TIME

"That wasn't funny!" Christina scolded Grant at space camp headquarters. "You scared the asteroids out of me!"

Grant replied calmly, "The Gallery of Planets is like outer space. There's no air in outer space, we weren't wearing spacesuits, so I couldn't breathe. Besides, I was ready for a snack!"

Slumped in a chair, Junko was playing absentmindedly with her shoelaces. Christina thought she had never seen anyone look so sad. The boys noticed, too.

"I bet she feels badly about the way she treated you," Christina whispered. "I think we should give her another chance to be our friend. Let's tell her about the clue. And Grant, you need to apologize."

"Apologize?" Grant asked, making a face. "I didn't mean to hit her!"

"Apologize anyway," Christina said.

Christina smiled at Junko. "How are you feeling?" she asked.

"Fine," Junko said with a puzzled look. She turned back to her shoelace game.

"Sorry I hit you with a planet," Grant managed to say with a weak smile.

"Well, you shouldn't be such a klutz," was Junko's hasty reply.

Christina bit her tongue. She refused to get into another argument and plopped down on a rug beside Grant and Phillip. Todd tossed each of them a strange silver pouch.

"What's this?" Grant asked Todd.

"The drink of astronauts," he answered grandly, "Tang."

Grant shook the pouch. "Seems kinda dry," he said and frowned.

"Astronauts on the Gemini missions first used it," Todd explained. "Their water was a byproduct of the life support system, and it didn't taste good. Tang powder made it tasty. Of course, it had to be mixed in zero-gravity pouches so the granules wouldn't fly all over the space capsule."

Todd demonstrated the process. "Now, squeeze it into your mouth," he said.

Grant squeezed with gusto, sending a geyser of orange liquid shooting to the ceiling. He quickly stuck out his tongue to catch a taste of the falling orange droplets. "Like orange juice, but not exactly," he said, ignoring the groans of everyone else now drenched in orange stickiness.

Christina could not stand feeling sticky. She made a beeline for the bathroom, closed the door and was about to wash her arms when the fast and steady

Click Click
Clop Clop
Click
Clop

of boot heels in the hallway made her freeze. It was the same sound Papa's cowboy boots made on a hard floor. *Has he come to pick us up early?* Christina wondered. *Is something wrong?* She leaned over just as the boots paused in front of the wide crack under the bathroom door. They weren't Papa's. Christina saw the glimmer of gold metal caps on the toes!

9

ASTRO DAD!

Christina held her breath and watched the bathroom doorknob slowly turn. She was about to yell, "OCCUPIED!" when the knob stopped moving. She strained to hear voices whispering feverishly, but couldn't make out the words. The boot heels suddenly

CLIP CLOPPED

back down the hall as quickly as they had come. She had heard two people whispering, but only one set of feet leaving.

Is someone outside waiting to grab me? she fretted. There was only one way to find out. Christina got on her stomach and slithered to the door. She pressed her cheek against the cold, hard tile and peeked underneath.

Straining her eyes in both directions, she saw nothing but empty hallway.

Christina didn't know why she was so worried. Lots of men in Texas wear cowboy boots. They did look a lot like Kent's, but he was at the ranch with Mimi and Papa, or at least he was supposed to be there.

After washing up, Christina joined Grant and Phillip who were discussing the clue.

"What could MGA mean and how could people race to the moon?" Grant asked no one in particular.

Junko, who had not moved from her chair, released a loud sigh.

"What do you think, Junko?" Christina asked.

"Don't you know anything about space history?" asked Junko. "The United States and Russia raced each other to the moon. Each country wanted to be the first to get there. The United States won, of course."

"If you're so smart, then what does MGA spell?" Grant asked, after taking a long slurp from a fresh space pouch of Tang.

"It could stand for all the missions during the space race—*Mercury, Gemini,* and *Apollo,*" Junko answered.

It was time for Christina to ask Junko the question she had wanted to ask since they met. "How do you know so much about the space program?"

"I've grown up in the space program," she answered. "My father is an astronaut."

Tang spewed out of Grant's mouth like fire from a rocket. Christina and Phillip, once again showered with orange rain, stared at her, dumbfounded.

"Can we meet him?" Grant asked excitedly after he wiped his mouth on his arm.

"That would be impossible," Junko said. "He's been on the Space Station for the past six months working on important energy experiments."

"That is *soooo* cool!" Christina exclaimed.

"Yeah," Junko agreed. "But I sure do miss him. He's supposed to come home on the next shuttle mission. I hope he makes it in time for my birthday next week."

Now Christina understood why Junko was so cranky. She couldn't imagine having her father floating high above the earth for months at a time.

The sound of shattering glass made the kids jump.

"Call security!" Todd yelled. "They've escaped!"

10

MERCURY MEN

The kids were relieved when they saw the "escapees." Todd, tiptoeing gingerly among shards of broken glass, was trying to corral crickets—hundreds of them.

"Hey, Todd," Grant called. "Are you going fishing?"

Todd pushed his moppy hair out of his eyes and flashed Grant an angry look. "You'll find out about the crickets later!" he bellowed. "Explore the Space Center and we'll meet back in an hour for a space lunch."

"Let's go to the Kid's Space Place!" Grant suggested. He pointed eagerly at the colorful structure that included rocket ships and space stations where kids were exploring mazes and zooming down giant slides.

"Great idea," Christina agreed. "Why don't you and Phillip check it out?" But Christina wanted to learn about the *Mercury* missions. "Junko, will you come with me?" she asked.

"Gladly!" Junko said, relieved she didn't have to spend time with the boys.

Seven *Mercury* astronauts wearing shiny silver space suits were featured at one display. "They look like they're wrapped in aluminum foil, just like Mimi's Thanksgiving turkey," Christina said, and laughed.

She learned that Alan Shepard became the first American in space on May 5, 1961, aboard the spacecraft *Freedom 7*. The flight lasted only about 15 minutes. A year later, John Glenn was the first astronaut to orbit the earth. He went around three times. But Christina didn't see anything that looked like a clue.

"Do you want to see a real piece of the *Mercury* program?" Junko asked. She led Christina to a grimy, brown space capsule marked *Faith 7*. Astronaut Gordon Cooper orbited the earth 22 times in the tiny capsule.

"It looks like a big Hershey's kiss without the wrapper," Christina said, disappointed the door was closed. "Wish we could see inside."

"The early space capsules weren't very big because they had no way to land and had to splash down into the ocean with parachutes," Junko explained.

Christina couldn't imagine a man cramped in there, much less falling back into the ocean from space. Suddenly, she noticed that someone had marked on the information plaque.

"I can't believe someone would do that!" she said angrily. Christina pulled a tissue from her pocket to clean it off—then stopped. It was hard to make out, but the marks were words! She and Junko worked to **decipher** the writing. It said:

HAM KNOWS

"How could a ham know anything?" Christina asked. "It tastes great, but it doesn't think. How could this possibly be a clue?"

11

MONKEY BUSINESS

When the boys joined them, Christina told them about the clue. Grant had the answer. "It means it's time for us to go find a ham sandwich," he said. "I'm starving!" He leaned over the metal rail surrounding the *Faith 7*, lost his balance, and flipped over, slamming his shoes into the capsule.

GONG!

"Stop monkeying around, Grant," Christina warned. "You're going to get us kicked out of camp before we solve this mystery."

Junko got a gleam in her eye. "Monkeys— that's it!" she said. "Before men went into space, they sent animals into space as part of the *Mercury* program. They wanted to see if animals could survive weightlessness in space before they risked humans. Russia sent a dog. The U.S. sent mice, monkeys, and chimps. Ham was the first chimpanzee in space!"

"Let's see if we can find something about him," Christina exclaimed.

They pushed their way through a group of foreign tourists speaking a language that Grant decided was Russian.

"What if they're spies?" he asked. "I'd better tail them and make sure they don't have a plot to steal American space secrets."

"It's OK, Grant," said Christina with a smirk. We won the space race decades ago and now U.S. and Russian astronauts work together on the Space Station along with astronauts from many other countries. But," she added sarcastically, "if you see anyone with a big rock that looks like your nose, let me know."

Soon, Christina spotted a small display about Ham. "He's so cute!" she said.

"A cute little ape, just like your brother," teased Junko.

Grant scratched under his arms and made loud chimp noises. "OOH! OOH! AHH! AHH!"

Christina ignored her brother's antics.

"In 1961, Ham reached an altitude of 157 miles and a speed of 5,857 miles-per-hour before splashing down in the ocean," she read. "He was tired and dehydrated, but he survived."

She noticed the plaque had the same mysterious marks. "We're on the right track!" she said. "Help me figure this out."

Christina pulled out her space pen to jot it down: PASS SATURN AND GET TO THE POINT.

A loud and creepy

CREEEAAAK

made the kids spin around. The door of the
Faith 7 capsule was now open! *Had someone
been hiding inside?* Christina wondered. *Did
someone hear them discussing the clues?*

12

GRANT MOONWALKER

Todd seemed to appear out of nowhere when he rounded the HAM display. "I've been looking for you," he said, pulling up the strap of his backpack that had fallen off his shoulder. "What brought you way over here?"

"Just curiosity," Christina said, looking up at an astronaut mannequin floating above them. "What's that about?"

"That represents one of the important milestones of the *Gemini* missions," Todd explained. "Those missions came after *Mercury* and before *Apollo*. During the second manned *Gemini* mission, *Gemini IV* stayed in space for four days. During that time, astronaut Edward White performed the first spacewalk by an American. This was something important they had to learn to do before landing on the moon."

"I don't know how to spacewalk, but I can moon walk," Grant said. He shuffled his feet and pumped his arms in a backwards dance. Everyone around him giggled.

"You know those athletic shoes you're wearing were made for moon walking, don't you?" Todd asked.

"No, I just got them at the mall," Grant said, confused.

"I mean many things have improved because of the space program," said Todd, "including shoes. The process and materials for space shoes used on the moon were also used to improve athletic shoes on Earth. Another example is cordless tools. Every tool the astronauts used had to be battery-powered."

"Makes sense," Grant said. "I guess there's no extension cord long enough to reach the moon!"

Todd didn't laugh. "I have a treat for you after lunch," he said.

"Ice cream?" Phillip asked.

"No," Todd answered. "A shuttle launch!"

"Will we be the launcher or the launchee?" Grant asked.

"You'll see," Todd promised. "Now follow me to the Zero G Diner for some space grub."

Above the constant din of tourist chatter, Christina heard the distinct and rapid sound of cowboy boots.

Click Clop Click
Clop
Click
Clop

Her imagination launched into orbit and her focus was not on where she was walking.

WHAP!

Christina ran right smack into an astronaut in full space suit. Fortunately, the puffy white suit cushioned the blow. "Excuse me," Christina said, red faced. She looked up at the gold face shield and saw nothing but her own embarrassed reflection. The astronaut simply waddled past silently.

As the group cut through the Gallery of Astronauts, Grant was shocked when he looked at one of the space suit display tubes. "The one I saw move the day the rock was stolen is missing!" he exclaimed.

13

HOUSTON, WE HAVE A PROBLEM

Outside, the Houston heat and humidity slapped Christina in the face like a wet, soggy glove. A tram waited to transport them to the nearby Johnson Space Center. Christina squeezed in beside Grant.

"What's that?" she asked, when something poked her in the side.

Grant pulled out the robot claw Papa had bought him at the gift shop. "Astronauts should always be prepared!" he said, and snapped at his sister's neck.

While Space Center Houston was a fun place to learn *about* the space program, Johnson Space Center was a working part *of* the space program, where men and women learned to be astronauts. This was where scientists and engineers had directed the historic moon missions and now it was the mission control center for the space shuttle program.

When they passed through the gate for a chain link fence topped with three rows of razor-sharp barbed wire, Christina knew this was the real deal!

"What's that *GI*-normous building?" Grant asked, as they passed rockets from past launches that hulked like frozen statues in the grassy park.

"Inside's a *Saturn V* rocket lying on its side," Junko said. "If it was standing up it would be 30 stories tall!"

"*Saturn* rocket?" Christina asked, thinking of the clue: PASS SATURN AND GET TO THE POINT. Maybe the clue didn't mean the planet; maybe it meant the rocket! And don't rockets have points on the end? "Junko, what was the *Saturn* rocket used for?" Christina asked.

"It's the most powerful machine ever made—the type of rocket that took the *Apollo* missions to the moon," Junko answered.

"*Mercury, Gemini, Apollo,*" Christina said. "The third leg of the space race. We've got to go to the point of that rocket to find our next clue. I just know it!"

"OK, OK," Junko said. "But first we have to watch the shuttle launch. This shuttle is headed to the International Space Station to bring my dad home!"

When the tram stopped, Todd announced, "Before the shuttle launch, we're visiting the historic mission control room."

Inside, Christina shared the excitement Mimi had felt as the control room screen replayed historic scenes from the *Apollo 11* mission when astronaut Neil Armstrong first stepped onto the moon.

Junko had heard it all before and could hardly sit still. "Maybe they'll show us a live picture of my dad on the Space Station," she whispered hopefully to Christina.

Soon, Todd motioned it was time to go to the Shuttle Flight Control Room. From the glass observation area, the kids saw rows of long desks that corralled men and women staring intently at computers. Many chattered constantly in a curious language of space terms as their eyes darted across **complex** diagrams. One man kept thumbing through a manual as big as a New York City telephone book.

On a large screen, the kids watched the astronauts in bright orange suits buckling up in the shuttle, or orbiter, as the space pros call it, at Cape Canaveral, Florida. Through the speakers, their voices sounded like robots.

Another screen showed the Space Station.

Junko cried.

"Wow, he's got funny looking hair," Grant observed.

"There's not much gravity on the Space Station and that causes his hair to stick up," Christina said. "Your hair always looks like you're in *zero* gravity."

"Yep," Grant said, rubbing his unruly curls.

"What's zero gravity?" Phillip asked.

"It's when things are not held down by the gravitational pull of the earth," Christina explained. "Like when Grant took the lid off the blender when Mimi was mixing a milkshake. It blasted all over the ceiling."

Junko looked as nervous as Christina had felt when she was on the simulator. Christina could see tiny beads of sweat above Junko's lip as she squeezed the arms of her seat and waited anxiously for the countdown. Finally, it came:

5
4
3 2
1...

LIFTOFF!!!

Everyone in the viewing area, including Christina, gasped. Mission control members clapped high fives. Red, orange, and blue flames surged from the shuttle's engines and white-hot exhaust from the solid rocket boosters pushed out thunderstorm-sized clouds. The mammoth white orbiter rested on the massive orange external fuel tank like a butterfly on a tree as it shot skyward. The white exhaust clouds soon became a column in the brilliant blue sky, pushing the shuttle higher and higher until it was a tiny speck with a long fluffy tail of smoke.

"That was incredible," Christina said. She heard Junko let out a deep breath like a party balloon losing its air. "Aren't you happy, Junko? The shuttle's on its way to bring your dad home!"

"There are so many things that could cause delays," she said. "I don't think he'll be here for my birthday." Junko's eyes teared. Embarrassed that Christina noticed, she added, "In space, no one can see you cry because the tears don't flow."

"What did you think of the launch?" Christina asked Grant. "Grant?" Her little brother was not in his seat. Neither was Phillip. "Houston, we have a problem!" Christina said, perplexed.

14

GETTING TO THE POINT

"I'll let Todd know that Grant and Phillip are missing," Junko said.

"No!" Christina cried. "The last thing we need to do is get security involved. Let's look for them ourselves."

"Won't Todd notice that we have all disappeared?" Junko asked.

"It looks like he's occupied," Christina said, pointing at a gaggle of kids who had cornered Todd to ask if they could go to the bathroom or get a snack.

Slipping quickly out of the control room, Junko led Christina into a maze of hallways. Junko moved confidently, knowing which hallways led to exits. Christina paused briefly to glance at a painting of one of the Apollo launches. When she looked up, Junko had vanished. The hallway forked and Christina had no clue which way to go! She heard elevator doors screech open, and hoped someone would come out—someone who could help her find her way. She raced down the hallway to catch the elevator occupant, and then froze. The person who emerged was the man in the blue jumpsuit— the man who had snatched the crumpled clue from her earlier.

I'll bet he knows we're on to something, Christina thought. Her heart did somersaults in her chest and she wished Mimi and Papa were not so far away.

"Are you lost?" the man asked, grinning like a model in a toothpaste commercial. Christina noticed the yellow pad in his pocket, covering his name patch. It was the same kind of paper as the note.

"No," Christina answered nervously. "My friends are around the corner. I stopped to look at that painting."

"One of my favorites," he said, nodding at the painting. "You'd better be careful around here."

Was his advice concern or a threat? Christina wondered. She waited quietly to make sure the coast was clear and peeked into the hallway. It wasn't. Running feet made her heart pound. Had the blue jumpsuit man alerted security?

"I turned around and she was gone!" Christina heard a familiar voice say. She peeked again and saw Junko, Grant, and Phillip running down the hall.

"Wait, you guys!" she yelled.

Sneakers squealed as they all stopped in their tracks and spun around. Junko explained that she ran right into Grant and Phillip when she rounded a corner, but then realized she'd lost Christina.

"What were you doing?" Christina asked Grant as she grabbed his bony shoulders.

"Bathroom break," he answered. "You were so mesmerized by the launch; I knew I couldn't get your attention."

Christina spotted the red glow of an exit sign at the end of the dim hallway. "Since we're already probably in trouble, we might as well look for the clue," she suggested. "Let's go!"

In Rocket Park, some rockets stood like skyscrapers while others napped on the ground.

Inside the "gi-normous" building Grant had noticed earlier, the *Saturn V* rocket lay on its side like a sleeping black and white giant. The rocket was divided into the different sections it would have separated into during a mission.

"Someone could actually live here," Grant said, staring at the cone-shaped boosters on the rocket's back end.

"Hello!" he yelled up at the giant cone closest to   him.

"Helllooo!"

the echo replied.

The kids raced beside the giant rocket like tiny ants running beside a fallen log.

Grant stopped long enough to admire an engine on one of the sections. "When I get my first car, it's going to have an engine like this one!" he said.

Finally reaching the top of the rocket, Junko spotted something fluttering from the tip. "There's a tiny flag hanging from the point!" she exclaimed. It was the first time Christina had seen her smile.

But when Christina saw the flag hanging high above their heads, it was her turn to be discouraged. "There's no way we can reach that."

"Yes, there is!" said Junko. "What if someone climbed on top of the rocket?"

"Who could we get to do that?" Grant asked innocently.

Christina and Junko smiled.

"How about you?" Junko asked. "I saw a ladder on the side."

Christina and Junko made a stirrup with their hands and gave Grant a leg up. His fingers barely reached the bottom rung, but those rock walls he liked to climb at the gym had been good practice.

Phillip watched for security guards as the girls kept an eye on Grant.

Grant quickly scurried to the top. Christina was amazed at the sight of her small brother, arms outstretched, walking along the top of the goliath rocket like it was a balance beam.

"Careful, Grant," Christina warned. When he reached the metal rods that met at the rocket's point, Grant got on his belly and slid as close as he could. He stretched his arm, but the flag was still out of reach. Red-faced and frustrated, he shrugged at Christina. He grinned and tapped his temple in an "I'm so smart!" motion. Grant reached for the back of his belt and pulled out his robot claw. He snagged the flag off the rocket's tip and stuffed it in his pocket. His feet sounded like drum beats running down the rocket's back.

Christina and Junko took their positions and helped Grant to the ground. After they galloped outside, Grant pulled the little flag out of his pocket. It read:

"What does that mean, Junko?" he asked.

"I don't have a clue!" she said, frustrated.

"Why the long faces?" Christina asked. "We're Americans. We put a man on the moon. Don't you think we can find a rock?"

"We should remember *Apollo 13*," Junko said.

"What happened?" Grant asked.

"An oxygen tank exploded on the way to the moon," Junko explained. "The crew could have died from carbon monoxide poisoning, but they worked together, built an air scrubber and splashed down safely."

"Yeah—teamwork!" Christina exclaimed. "Let's blast off in search of our next clue!"

"Hold it right there!" a deep voice ordered.

Christina's confidence quickly turned to fear.

15

LIVING IN SPACE

After the blistering Houston heat, the air-conditioned Living in Space Module back at Space Center Houston felt like heaven.

"How do they go to the bathroom?" Grant asked, as Todd described life for the astronauts on the Space Station.

Christina wasn't surprised that her brother would ask this question. She was thankful Todd hadn't realized they'd been missing and that the security guard who frightened them in the rocket park thought they were simply lost. Unfortunately, they had missed break time and now she was exhausted and hungry.

To Christina's embarrassment, Grant wasn't finished with his question.

"I mean, when astronauts use the bathroom doesn't everything that comes out just float up into the air?" he continued.

"GROSS!!!"

came a chorus of camper voices.

"It's a fair question," Todd said. "Even the astronauts would float off the toilet if they didn't strap themselves on! Plastic bags are placed in the toilet for solid wastes and the bags are sucked down into a holding tank. Liquid wastes are handled in different ways. Sometimes, they're flushed into space where they're vaporized. Surprisingly, liquid wastes can also be recycled into drinking water."

The kids cried out again:

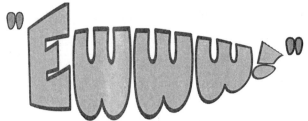

"Sometimes astronauts do the same thing babies do—wear diapers," Todd said. "During long space walks, there's no other choice. It's also hard to take showers on the Space Station, since the water floats instead of falling straight down as it does on Earth," Todd continued. "Many astronauts prefer to take sponge baths."

"Do they have a washing machine up there?" Phillip asked.

"No, they don't," Todd said. "And most astronauts only change underwear every three or four days!"

"Mimi would have a hissy fit if I did that!" Grant whispered.

"Dirty clothes and garbage are always a problem on the Space Station. One creative astronaut used his dirty underwear to grow seeds. But now there's a new automated transfer vehicle that's fired into space on a rocket and docks with the Space Station. It takes supplies to the Space Station and when it's emptied, garbage and dirty clothes are placed inside. It burns up as it re-enters the earth's atmosphere, so it looks like a shooting star."

Christina laughed loudly. "When you make a wish on a shooting star, you might be wishing on dirty underwear!"

"Where do the astronauts sleep?" a girl in the back asked.

"The astronauts can really sleep anywhere in the Space Station as long as they attach their sleeping bags to the wall and zip themselves in," Todd replied. "If they didn't do that, they would just float around."

"Could that be the kind of bag our clue was talking about?" Christina whispered to Junko.

"It might be!" Junko agreed.

"Somehow we've got to see inside those sleeping bags," Christina said. "When the other kids leave, let's stay at the end of the line so Todd won't notice what we're doing."

As Todd led the campers out, Christina and the others stayed in the shadows until they heard the door close.

"Everybody pick a sleeping bag and start looking for clues!" Christina said.

Grant couldn't resist getting inside one of the bags and zipping up. "Look at me, I'm an astronaut," he said.

"You look more like a sack of potatoes with blond hair," Christina teased. "Did anybody find anything?"

"I turned this one inside out and there was nothing," Phillip said.

"Nothing here," said Junko.

"I haven't found anything either," Christina said, disappointed. "What about you, Grant?"

Grant just snored.

Christina noticed the light in the module slowly fading, as if a battery was getting weak. "Hurry, Grant, check your bag for a clue," she said. "Stop fooling around."

Grant reached down into the bag, becoming a bumpy lump inside it. "I feel something!" he exclaimed.

"Grab it and let's get out of here," Christina said, as the darkness closed around them.

They felt their way to the shiny metal door. Christina gave it a twist and pulled.

"It's locked!" she cried in horror.

16

SPACE BOOGERS

After waiting hours for Todd to realize that they were missing and rescue them from the locked module, the kids zipped into sleeping bags. Junko and Phillip were soon asleep.

"Christina, you awake?" Grant whispered.

"Yeah," she replied.

"I wish Mimi and Papa were here," he said.

"Me, too," she answered.

"Want a space food stick?" he asked.

"No thanks, Grant. I thought you were saving those for school," she answered, her eyelids growing heavy.

"This is an emergency," he said.

The next thing Christina knew, a loud **commotion** and a bright light woke her up.

"There you are!" Todd yelled furiously. "I've been looking for you all night! Do you want me to lose my job? Give me one reason I shouldn't send you home right now!"

Christina didn't have a reason, and a part of her secretly wished she was home—or at least with Mimi and Papa. Instead she gave him her most innocent look and said, "Sorry."

Todd's next question surprised her. "You didn't bother anything or see anything unusual, did you?" he asked.

"It was too dark and scary in here to do anything but sleep," Christina answered.

"If I catch you kids somewhere you shouldn't be again, it will mean a one-way ticket out of here," Todd cautioned. "Now follow me. We're headed to the shuttle mock-up."

"I sure could use some breakfast," Grant said, and yawned.

"You missed breakfast," Todd said sternly.

After their ordeal, Christina had forgotten all about their mission. "Grant!" she said. "Did you look at what you found in your sleeping bag?

"I forgot!" he said, fishing in his pocket. He pulled out a business card. "That's strange," Grant said. "It's a business card for Roberts Spacey Collectibles." He flipped the card over and saw something scribbled on the back:

floating
will help
you see

"The rock thief is probably selling the moon rock to the space collectibles company," Grant observed.

"But what is the floating part about?" Christina pondered.

The shuttle mock-up looked like a shuttle had crashed through the rear wall of Space Center Houston.

"The space shuttle's nose is almost as big as yours!" Grant teased Christina. He ran his fingers over the shuttle's white tiles. "It feels like Papa's foam ice chest!"

"More than 21,000 heat insulating tiles cover the shuttle," Todd explained. "Each one has a unique shape."

"Sounds like that big jigsaw puzzle we did," Grant commented.

"The tiles protect the shuttle when it re-enters Earth's atmosphere," added Todd. "It gets as hot as volcano lava!"

On the shuttle flight deck, Grant and Phillip slipped into the commander and pilot seats.

"We're in the shuttle's nose," Grant snickered. "I guess that makes us space boogers!"

Phillip threw his head back and laughed.

Grant and Phillip furiously jiggled the shuttle joysticks. "Coming in for a landing..." Grant pretended.

"Time's up, guys!" Todd shouted. When he turned to leave the cockpit, his ever-present backpack hit the door's edge.

That's odd, Christina thought. *Backpacks shouldn't clank!*

17

ROVING ROCKET

"Divide into teams of four," Todd barked as he handed out long white boxes. "Each box contains the parts you will need to construct a rocket. Read the instructions and measure carefully."

Working together, Christina's team finished first. The red and white rocket was almost as tall as Grant.

"Good job!" said Todd. "Now, here's your astronaut."

The kids were dumbfounded as they watched Todd unscrew the rocket's clear top and place a cricket inside.

"So that's what the crickets are for!" Grant exclaimed.

"Poor little thing," Christina said. "He doesn't even have a helmet!"

"Let's name him Cricket Ham in honor of Ham the chimpanzee astronaut," Junko suggested.

Todd placed the rocket in a circle of crushed gravel that reminded Christina of the moon's surface.   Everyone put on astronaut helmets and took cover behind a concrete wall. Todd lit the rocket's fuse.

"BLAST OFF!"

The rocket shot skyward like fireworks on the Fourth of July.   It corkscrewed into the air, leaving a curly smoke tail until it was a tiny dot in the bright Texas sky. When its red and white parachute popped to deliver the rocket's capsule safely to earth, a sudden wind gust blew it off course.

"It's not coming back!" Grant yelled. "We've got to rescue Cricket Ham!"

Todd was occupied launching another rocket, so the kids slipped behind a long row of bushes to follow the rapidly drifting parachute.

BLAST OFF!

"We'll never catch it on foot," Grant whined. "Can't we use those?" He pointed at a couple of odd vehicles that looked like six-legged bugs with wheels.

"Must be the new experimental rovers NASA is testing for future moon missions," Junko said.

"Let's check 'em out!" Grant shouted. He and Phillip climbed on a rover.

"Grant, you shouldn't!" Christina warned.

"It has video games!" Grant exclaimed.

"Those aren't video games!" Junko cautioned when Grant started punching buttons.

"Grant, stop!" Christina yelled when the rover started rolling. It topped a grassy hill and quickly gained speed.

"There's only one way to catch them!" a panicked Christina said. Junko nodded and they climbed on the other rover, quickly fastening the helmets they found on the seat. Junko feverishly pushed buttons until the rover lurched forward. Christina pushed the accelerator pedal and struggled to steer the rover, which bounced like it was traveling on the crater-pocked lunar surface.

They were gaining on Grant and Phillip when the rocket started its descent. Grant yelled, "How do you stop this thing?" He turned sharply and cut right in front of Christina.

The rovers collided! Christina and Junko's helmeted heads slammed hard against the metal frame.

Grant and Phillip slowly removed their helmets. Grant's face was white as baby powder and his damp curls were glued to his head. "That's one way to stop!" he said sheepishly.

"I think the rocket landed behind that building," Phillip added in a quivering voice.

"Let's go," Christina said, rubbing her sore head. She wondered what would happen to them when NASA discovered the wrecked moon rovers that probably cost a bazillion dollars!

"Oh, no!" cried Grant when he found the rocket parachute in a pile of gray rocks. "It's cracked and Cricket Ham is missing!"

Chirp! Chirp!

"There you are!" Christina said, gently lifting the brave insect and placing him on a soft patch of grass. A white ticket fluttering between two rocks attracted her attention. "It's a pass to the Neutral **Buoyancy** Lab, whatever that is," she said. Only then did she notice that the two rocks looked an awful lot like moon rocks!

18

ONE SMALL STEP

"Hey!" Grant said, inspecting the rocks. "They're all the same!" He smashed one rock against another. It cracked like an eggshell. "It's hollow!" he said, surprised.

"What's this stuff?" Phillip asked and pointed to pile of powdery gray dust.

"I don't know," Junko said. "But two people stepped in it."

One large footprint was like one they had seen many times before—the famous first step on the moon. The other print was more down to earth—a cowboy boot.

"Looks like an astronaut and a cowboy are mixed up in this rock ruckus!" Grant said. "But what are they up to?"

Before anyone could offer an opinion, a shout startled them all. "There they are!" Three astronauts in full space suits raced toward the rovers.

"We'd better get out of here!" Christina said.

They dashed to the nearest building and dove through a door. Inside the door was an area as black as space.

"That was close," Grant said with a long sigh.

"Shhh!" Christina said. "Someone could have followed us."

Almost on cue, the door opened, and then slammed. The kids held their breath.

The determined footsteps were heading toward them!

"Let's feel our way along the wall until we find another door," Christina whispered frantically. Soon, she felt the cold metal of a door handle. Gingerly, she turned it and prayed it wouldn't creak. They slipped blindly into a room crammed full of equipment.

"Ouch!" Grant mumbled, hitting his shin on a hard edge.

Christina found some sort of bench. "Over here," she said softly. The kids cowered together, listening for the boots. They moved closer and closer, then stopped.

CH-ssssssshhhhh

CH-sssssssssshhhhhh

CH-sssssssshhhhhhhh

Their seat, whatever it was, was coming to life. Slowly it began to spin. "Better hold on!" Christina ordered.

The slow-motion ride quickly got faster and faster, until Christina felt like a sock tumbling around in a clothes dryer.

"We're on a centrifuge!" Junko cried.

Christina knew that was a machine that spun astronauts to prepare them for space flight. She felt like she was about to lose her lunch.

Finally, the centrifuge started slowing and then stopped.

"Are we still spinning?" Grant asked in a groggy voice. "I wish I had on one of those space diapers!"

"Shhhh!" Christina warned. Outside the door, the boots walked past and the kids heard someone laughing.

Christina no longer doubted that the rock thief, or thieves, knew the kids were on their trail. *Did the boots belong to Kent? More importantly, were Mimi and Papa safe at the ranch?*

19

UNDERWATER SPACE

The four dizzy friends locked arms and stumbled out of the dark building. Outside, sunshine blinded them. "I can't walk all the way back," Grant whined, dragging his feet.

"Me either," Phillip agreed.

"Maybe that bus goes to the Neutral Buoyancy Lab," Junko suggested when she saw the NASA bus stop nearby.

They scrambled onto the bus and settled in their seats. Christina didn't notice the clue-snatching custodian sitting in the back seat.

"Next stop, Neutral Buoyancy Lab," the driver said.

"What's the lab used for?" Christina asked Junko.

"It's the largest man-made pool in the world," Junko said. "Water makes you weightless, like being in space, so astronauts train in it."

"You mean they float in it!" Christina said. "That's what the clue on the business card meant:

floating
will help
you see

I'll bet there's a clue in the pool!"

Inside the Buoyancy Lab, Christina marveled at the pool's size while she waited for the others to return from the restroom. The pool gleamed like an indoor lake and in the deep water, astronauts worked in slow motion on a Space Station mock-up.

"Lost again?" a deep voice asked.

Christina turned to see the custodian.

"No," she answered, frowning. She glanced at his feet hoping to see cowboy boots. He was wearing sneakers. He stopped long enough to pick up a gum wrapper and toss it in a trash can before scrambling away.

Junko, Phillip, and Grant returned with a lady in a wetsuit.

"Christina, this is my dad's friend,Charlotte," Junko said. "She's one of the divers who help the astronauts train underwater. She's trying to get an OK for us to try on a space suit and get in the pool!"

"No promises, Junko," Charlotte cautioned. "But I'll see what I can do."

In a few minutes, Charlotte waved the kids over. "I pulled some strings," she told Junko. "You and one friend can get in the pool for a few minutes."

Christina, Grant, and Phillip looked eagerly at Junko. To everyone's surprise she said, "Grant, would you like to come? I was so nasty to you when we first met, I'd like to make it up to you."

Christina was disappointed, but happy to see Junko's kindness to her brother. "Don't forget to look for clues," she reminded them.

Junko and Grant looked like inflated character balloons in the Macy's Thanksgiving Day Parade in their astronaut suits. A platform lowered them slowly into the water. Bubbles rose like those from a fizzy drink as they sank to the bottom of the 40-foot-deep pool. Divers hovered to help them. Christina and Phillip, watching from the viewing area, waved crazily.

When Christina looked up, she spied the custodian pulling on a helmet and sliding into the water. "He might be our rock thief!" she told Phillip. "And I'm afraid he might try to hurt Grant and Junko!"

"What can we do?" Phillip asked.

"You wait here," Christina said. She slipped out of the viewing area and scrambled around the pool. When she reached the oxygen lines attached to the astronauts training underwater—including her brother and Junko—she wasn't sure which one to disconnect.

She frantically made her choice and pulled with all her might until the hose popped off the oxygen machine. A column of bubbles rose and

Ready for a "space swim"!

divers helped someone to the surface. When they pulled the helmet off, Christina was relieved. It was the custodian.

"What happened?" he asked the divers who pulled him from the pool.

Before Christina could hear the answer, a security guard dashed toward her. She thought he was coming to arrest the custodian. Instead, he headed straight for her!

"You can't leave the viewing area, Miss," he said gruffly.

"She gets lost a lot," the custodian said, and grinned at Christina.

Christina glared at him. "Don't you know who he is?" she ranted at the guard.

"Sure I do," he said with a laugh.

So that's it, Christina thought. *There are security guards involved.*

"I think you'd better come with me," the guard said.

"Wait!" Christina begged. Grant and Junko were splashing out of the pool.

"Let's go!" the guard ordered. Christina hung her head. *Should I make a run for it?* she wondered.

"I'll take custody of this one, sir," a familiar voice said.

Christina looked up. "Papa!" she shouted. "I'm so glad to see you!"

20

RESTING ROCK RANCH

"Is Mimi OK?" Christina asked, still concerned that Kent might be a rock wrangler.

"She's having a rodeo of a time!" said Papa, who noticed Christina's sad expression. "What's wrong, honey?"

"Just tired," Christina answered. She didn't confess that she'd never felt like such a failure. They were leaving space camp and hadn't solved the mystery!

Junko and Phillip, who'd gotten permission from their moms to attend the barbecue, hopped in the back seat with Christina and Grant.

During the ride to the ranch, the kids rehashed all that had happened.

"Did you see any possible clues in the pool?" Christina asked Junko and Grant.

"Nothing," Junko said sadly.

"I saw a strange little sign," Grant said. "It looked like gobbledygook—the letters were all backwards."

Christina handed Grant her space pen. She knew her brother's memory was amazing. "Why don't you try and write it for us?"

Grant concentrated to write what he had seen:

"That reminds me of those weird space suit labels," Christina said.

"I know about those," Junko said. "They're backwards because the astronauts can't bend their heads down to read them. They have to use mirrors attached to their wrists."

Christina unzipped her duffle bag and dug furiously. "Here!" she said, pulling out a small mirror. "Let's see if you're right."

"RESTING ROCK RANCH," she read from the reflection.

Christina shared her suspicions about the custodian and Kent. She hated suspecting Mimi's friend, but someone with gold-toed boots had definitely been after them. "What a coincidence," Christina said. "This clue mentions a ranch and we're headed for one. Something tells me we need to investigate Kent's office carefully!"

At the ranch, the smoky-sweet aroma of roasting pork wafted to the car and greeted the hungry kids.

"Kent may be a rock thief," Grant whispered. "But he sure knows how to barbecue."

After lots of annoying kisses on the cheek from the crowd of guests, the kids plopped down on bales of hay circling the barbecue pit. Judy passed out chips and spicy salsa.

"9-1-1! 9-1-1! My mouth's on fire!" Grant hollered after chomping down on a big chunk of jalapeno pepper.

Papa, in his dress jeans, white shirt, and red bow tie, twirled Mimi round and round in her red ruffled party dress while fiddlers played a fast reel. When Kent and Judy joined the dance, Christina saw their opportunity.

"Now's our chance!" she said.

The buffalo heads on the wall watched suspiciously as the kids slunk into Kent's dark office.

Junko shrieked when she accidentally laid her hand on an armadillo's head. "That's creepy!"

Christina tried each of the desk drawers. They were locked.

Click
Clop

The frightening sound of boots in the hallway sent the kids cowering under the desk. The boots walked past the office, but softer footsteps padded straight to the desk.

The kids held their breath. Christina's mind was racing! Her heart was pounding! *If only I could get a look!* she thought.

ZzzzzZZZip!

Christina could see Grant's blue eyes glowing like full moons at the sound. More followed.

CLINK!
SWOOSH-PLUNK!

ZzzzzZZZip!

Christina could stand it no longer. She leaned over for a peek. To her horror, her space pen rolled from her pocket and clattered across the wooden floor.

The mysterious prowler froze.

21

ROCKY RUCKUS

"Chris-ti-na! Gra-nt!" Papa was calling them. *Should they answer and put Papa in danger?* Christina fretted.

Grant already knew his answer. "In here, Papa!" he yelled.

Papa was there in a flash. "There's someone out here I want you to meet!" he said, flipping on the light.

The kids scrambled from their hiding place and dashed behind Papa, dumbfounded by someone standing before them in a space suit!

"Has this shindig moved inside?" Mimi asked as she and Kent entered the office. She stopped short when she saw the space man. "Oh, Kent! You hired an astronaut impersonator to surprise the kids!"

"They're surprised, all right," Papa said. "They're sticking to me like sand spurs in a horse's tail!"

"I didn't hire anyone," Kent said, confused.

Christina pointed to the metal stand. "Where'd you get that rock?" she asked Kent.

"That's a genu-*wine* imitation moon rock," Kent explained. "A neighboring rancher's son brought it to me a few days ago. It fit that old globe stand perfectly. "

Another man pushed his way into the office. Christina knew his face. It was the Space Center custodian!

"Hey!" he said with a brilliant grin. "I thought there was someone who wanted to meet me!"

"Uncle Bill?" Junko said.

"Hi Junko!" he said.

"You know him?" Christina asked. She suddenly realized that she had been alone each time she had encountered the custodian.

"He's my father's best friend, Colonel Bill Rodriguez," Junko replied. "I call him Uncle Bill. He's an astronaut."

"This is who I wanted you to meet!" Papa said.

The blood drained from Christina's face. "I thought you were a thief," she confessed. "Why did you snatch that paper out of my hand?"

"To throw it away for you," he said. "I'm a neat freak. I saw you pick it up."

"Would someone please explain what's going on?" Mimi asked, tapping her red high heel impatiently.

Christina stepped out. "We've caught a rock thief in the middle of a switcheroo!" she said. "Whoever's in that space suit stole a priceless moon rock from the Space Center!"

Christina's mind whirled, piecing together what had happened. "I think he was making copies of the rock," she said.

"The fake rocks we found!" Grant said.

"Yes, those were molds," Christina said. "The thief or thieves mixed that powder with water and poured it inside the molds. That way they could make lots of moon rocks to sell to collectors."

Christina picked up the rock on the desk and observed it carefully. "This one's a fake," she said, tossing it to Grant. "It looks like Grant's nose, but the booger's missing!"

Christina noticed the space man was holding a familiar backpack behind him. "Colonel Bill, if you'll remove this helmet, I think you'll find a space camp counselor named Todd!" she exclaimed.

The kids gasped.

Todd moved clumsily in the spacesuit and clutched the backpack with thick gloves. Kent wrestled it from his grip, just as Colonel Bill snatched the helmet off his head. Todd had a desperate look in his eyes.

"That's him!" Kent said. "He gave me the fake moon rock!"

"That was the real moon rock!" Christina exclaimed. "That was our last clue—the rock was resting at the ranch! He came here tonight to get it back and leave you with a fake. The real rock's in his backpack."

Just as Kent pulled out the real moon rock, Todd lunged, grabbed the rock and tossed it to a man in the back of the room. Boots CLIP CLOPPED lickety split to the front door and then stopped suddenly with a

The kids rushed into the hallway to see a man wearing fancy gold-toed boots, just like Kent's, spread-eagled and unconscious on the floor. He had tripped and hit his head on the moon rock!

"That's what I call 'a rock to the rescue!'" said Grant, giggling at his own joke.

22

MISSION ACCOMPLISHED!

During the next week, Christina and Grant read daily about the moon rock caper in the Houston paper. Reporters had learned that Todd was bitter after flunking out of astronaut school and had plotted with the man in the gold-toe boots to sell fake moon rocks. Todd had hidden the rock in the Space Center, moving it often to stay one step ahead of investigators and often disguising himself as an astronaut.

On their way to the airport to fly home, Mimi, Papa, Christina, and Grant had a stop to make—Junko's birthday party! Junko and Phillip were thrilled to see their fellow rock sleuths.

"If I ever become an astronaut like my dad," Junko said happily, "I want the three of you to be on my crew!"

"Yeah," Grant said. "Our friendship had a rocky start, but now it just rocks!"

"Make a wish," Christina said when Junko blew out the candles on her cake.

"I did!" Junko smiled.

About that time there was a knock at the door. Colonel Bill stuck his head in the room. "Can anyone come to this party?" he asked.

"Sure!" said Junko.

"Even this guy?" Colonel Bill swung the door wide open to reveal a man in a flight suit.

"Dad!" Junko screamed. She flew into her father's arms, and he wrapped her up in a loving bear hug.

After the happy reunion, Bill shared some good news with the moon rock hounds. "You'll be happy to know the moon rock is back where it belongs," he said. "Too bad about the reward."

"What reward?" Mimi asked.

"There was a reward for finding the moon rock, but then there was the little matter of the wrecked rovers," Colonel Bill explained.

"What rovers?" Mimi asked.

"Uh," Grant replied, "M-M-Mimi, let's talk about that later." He quickly changed the subject. "Papa, do you think we could strap some booster rockets on the *Mystery Girl*?"

"Yeah!" Christina agreed. "Then we'd always be ready to blast off at a moment's notice in search of another mystery!"

Now...go to

www.carolemarshmysteries.com
and...

- Add this book to your personal Adventure Map Tracker!

- Go on a Scavenger Hunt!

- Take a Pop(corn) Quiz!

- Hear from Mimi, Papa, Christina, and Grant!

- Talk to Christina and Grant!

- Join the Fan Club...and MUCH MORE!

GLOSSARY

astronaut: a person trained to pilot, navigate or participate in the flight of a spacecraft

centrifuge: a machine that simulates gravity

console: a panel that holds controls for electrical or mechanical equipment

docking: to join two or more spacecraft

kaleidoscope: a complex pattern of constantly changing colors and shapes

milestone: a significant event; or a sign on the side of the road to show distance

simulation: an imitation

SAT GLOSSARY

buoyancy: the tendency to remain afloat in a liquid or to rise in air or gas

clumsy: awkward movement

commotion: a disturbance

complex: complicated

decipher: to find out the meaning of

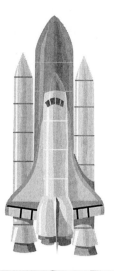

Space Center Houston TRIVIA

1. The footprints left by astronauts on the moon should last several million years!

2. The first "chimponaut" was a 3-year-old chimpanzee named Ham, who rocketed into space on January 31, 1961.

3. A space shuttle's main engine weighs about one seventh as much as a train engine but can deliver as much horsepower as 39 locomotives!

4. The black and white caps astronauts wear under their helmets are called "Snoopy" caps because they make the astronauts look like the famous comic strip character.

5. The bright orange space suits shuttle astronauts wear during launch and landing are called "pumpkin suits." They include life preservers, life rafts, smoke flares, emergency radios and even a signal mirror.

6. The word astronaut means "star sailor."

7. The first dog in space was a Russian dog named Laika.

8. The first American woman in space was Sally Ride.

9. The aircraft that produces short periods of weightlessness for astronauts in training is called the "Vomit Comet"!

Enjoy this exciting excerpt from:

THE MADCAP MYSTERY OF THE MISSING Liberty Bell

1 HOT GHOSTS?

Christina glanced nervously at the photograph in her hand and scanned the crowd once more. Her grandmother Mimi pulled a pair of red, rhinestone-studded sunglasses from her purse and parked them on her face.

"Think you'll recognize him when you see him?" she asked.

"I hope so," Christina answered, as she eyed her reflection in Mimi's flashy shades. "You know kids our age can change a lot in a year!"

Mimi nodded in agreement. Christina had grown two inches and had gotten braces since she sent Hunter her picture at the beginning of the school year.

Christina wondered if Hunter would look different from the photograph he sent her. Their classes had joined in a pen pal project to learn more about kids in other cities. She wrote him about her home in Peachtree City, Georgia, and all the history and sights of nearby Atlanta. Hunter wrote her about his hometown of Philly. That's what he called Philadelphia, Pennsylvania, the birthplace of the United States. Through their letters, they had become good friends.

When Hunter invited Christina and her younger brother Grant to visit, she worried...Hunter liked her letters, but would he like her in person?

Mimi, also known as mystery writer Carole Marsh, was all for it. "I've been planning a historical mystery!" she had said excitedly. "That'll be a great place for research! Papa and I would love to take you!"

After they settled on going several days before July 4th, Papa had agreed to fly them in his little red and white plane, *Mystery Girl*. He warned that the heat might be sweltering. He was right.

"Where's Papa with those snow cones already?" Mimi asked, impatiently tapping her red, high heel shoe on the old brick path. "You stay here and keep watching for Hunter while I find Papa and something cool!"

Christina mopped her upper lip with the tail of her green cotton blouse and wished she'd worn her favorite pink tank top instead. Along the meandering paths of Old City, the historical heart of Philadelphia, she saw heat waves dancing above the hot brick like shimmering ghosts. She imagined how hot the Founding Fathers must have been when they walked these paths in their powdered wigs, breeches, and stockings. It must have been even worse for the women in their long dresses and layers and layers of petticoats.

Suddenly, Christina felt a searing pain in her neck. "Ouch!" she yelped.

Are the ghostly figures I daydreamed about trying to get my attention? Christina wondered.

2

TOO MANY N'S

A muffled snicker caused Christina to whirl around. It was Grant! Standing behind her on a bench, he was directing a sunbeam on her neck with his jumbo magnifying glass.

She grabbed for it and yelled, "Are you trying to catch my ponytail on fire!?"

Grant dodged, hopped off the bench, and wove through tourists like a snake on a busy highway. Christina chased in hot pursuit, her long, chestnut-colored hair slipping out of its ribbon and flying wildly around her face.

She caught Grant's shirt, but tripped on a loose brick. Both slid across sprinkler-soaked grass.

"Give me that magnifying glass!" she ordered, wrestling it from his hands.

"Don't forget Philadelphia's nickname," Grant said between giggles. "You can't hurt me! We're in the City of Brotherly Love!"

Christina stood and held the magnifying glass triumphantly in the air, but suddenly realized she was a mess. Bits of grass and mud clung to her shirt and arms. Her white shorts had a grass stain Mr. Clean couldn't remove. And her hair stuck to her sweaty face like a spider web. She started to brush herself off when she felt a light tap on her shoulder.

"Christina, is that you?" a surprised voice asked.

Oh no! Christina's thoughts raced. Please don't let it be him! She turned, sheepishly. It was Hunter. He looked a lot like his picture—dark brown hair and big brown eyes.

"Wow!" Hunter said. "I knew you were interested in the Revolutionary War, but I didn't know you'd be fighting a battle!"

Christina's face was as red as Mimi's favorite hat. "Sorry I look this way," she stammered. "I had to take care of a little brother problem. It's great to finally meet you!"

She noticed Hunter had a girl with him. She had long brown hair and brown eyes. "You must be Hunter's neighbor, Isabella," Christina said.

"How did you know my name?" the girl asked.

"Hunter told me about you in his letters," said Christina.

Mimi and Papa stormed toward them with sticky snow cone juice dripping off their hands. "You're not where I left you!" Mimi said sternly. "But I see you found Hunter!"

"My dad's waiting for us at the Liberty Bell Center," Hunter said.

Papa licked his snow cone to stop the drips from making sticky dots on his cowboy boots. "Let's go," he said. "I'm melting faster than this snow cone!"

Outside the Liberty Bell Center, a long rectangular building with glass walls, Christina was surprised to see Hunter walk up to a tall man dressed like an American Revolutionary War soldier. When he took the musket rifle off his shoulder and held out a big hand to Christina, she realized it was Hunter's dad.

"I feel like I know you already!" he said. "Hunter has talked about you all year."

Christina blushed when she remembered how awful she looked.

"I've got to take part in an historical re-enactment," he continued. "Hunter can show you around Old City."

Enjoy this exciting excerpt from:

THE MYSTERY AT Fort Sumter

1 " WHAT FORT IS THIS?"

GRANT yawned. When the car stopped, he looked up to see that they were parked in front of what looked like a grand fortress.

"Are we going to sleep at Fort Sumter?" he asked, yawning again. He turned off his video player, thrusting the car from green gloom to just plain old black gloom.

"This is not Fort Sumter," said Papa, stretching, his cowboy hat scraping the roof. "This is a hotel. It's the old Citadel building, and yes, the young men who once stayed here would say it is indeed a fortress." Papa laughed.

From the back seat, Christina and Grant stared at the edifice shrouded in fogged light, then stared at each other. They shrugged their shoulders.

"Looks like a fort to me," Christina whispered to her brother.

"Towers...turrets...gun ports..." said Grant. "Yep, looks like a fort to me."

A GIANT yawn escaped from the front seat. "Are we sleeping at Fort Sumter?!" cried Mimi.

She stretched and sat straight up, her short blond hair a spiky mess.

"Oh, for gosh sakes!" moaned Papa. "It's a hotel! Or, we can sleep in the car."

"Uh, no thanks!" said Christina, shoving the Clemson afghan aside. She gathered her things. "There is no bathroom in the car."

"Or television," reminded Grant, eagerly grabbing his backpack.

Papa opened the car door as a sleepy bellman in a uniform approached. "No TV. It's late. It's bedtime. Let's go, pard'ners—NOW!"

The kids, and even Mimi, "hopped to."

"Wow," Christina whispered to her brother. "Papa sounds like a drill sergeant or something."

"He's just tired," said Mimi. "That drive in the sleet on the dark road is nerve-wracking."

"Mimi!" said Grant. "You were asleep...how do you know?"

Mimi turned around. Her eyes were still red from weeping over poor Aunt Lulu. "Now, Grant, you know how I have eyes in the back of my head?"

"Yes, ma'am," Grant said.

"Well, guess what?" said Mimi. "I can also 'backseat drive' your Papa from the front seat—even with my eyes closed."

Papa, who was holding her door open, shook his head. "It's true, Grant, and don't forget it. You can't get anything past Mimi." He gave Mimi a weary wink.

Mimi smiled and perked up. She hopped out of the car and followed the bellman and their luggage cart inside. Papa, Christina, and Grant followed obediently.

"Well, do we even get dinner?" Grant asked forlornly. He rubbed his tummy and tried to look like a starving waif. He and his sister waited eagerly for the answer.

Mimi and Papa barely turned their heads around, but together they said, "NO!"

As Christina entered the spooky, fortlike hotel, she noted the time on the lobby clock.

"Forgetaboutit, Grant," she said sadly, putting her arm around her brother's shoulders. "It's closer to breakfast than dinnertime. I have some M&Ms in my backpack. We'll make do."

"Great!" grumbled Grant. "Next, I guess we'll find out we're staying in the dungeon?"

Papa hovered over the check-in desk. A skeletal-looking desk clerk handed him a key. "The room you requested, sir," they overheard him say. "The Dungeon Suite."

Christina and Grant exchanged shocked glances, and nervously followed their grandparents into the gloom of the darkened lobby.